YOU CAN TEACH YOURSELF® GUITAR by EAR

By Mike Christiansen

CD CONTENTS

MEL BAY

Visit us on the Web at http://www.melbay.com — E-mail us at email@melbay.com

1 2 3 4 5 6 7 8 9 0

Contents

Introduction

"IF SOMEONE IS singing a song or playing a melody, how can I know what chords to play with it?" This is a common question often asked of guitar teachers and players by those who wish to play guitar by ear. This book will help you do just that. The material in this book will enable you to find the chords which sound good together. This will not only be helpful in playing by ear, but will help you write your own chord progressions and songs. You will learn many different accompaniment patterns (strumming, pick-strum, and fingerpicking styles) which can be used not only to play the exercises in this book, but they can be used to play thousands of songs by ear. If you're sitting around the campfire and everyone wants to sing and have you accompany them, if you want to learn a song from a recording, or if you want to write your own songs, the information in this book will make it possible. Each section of this book will help you with some aspect of playing by ear.

If you do not know some accompaniment patterns to use with music in 4/4 and 3/4, or if you want to learn some new patterns and styles, look in the appendix of this book for the sections on "Strum Patterns," "Pick-Strum Accompaniment Patterns," and "Finger-picking Patterns." These accompaniment styles can be applied to thousands of songs in 4/4, 3/4 and 6/8 time. Using these techniques to accompany the songs will provide continuity to the music, help the singer(s) to keep with the pulse of the music, and will also help you find where the chords should change. Although the emphasis of this book is to teach you to play by ear (without written music), the accompaniment styles are presented using measures. This will help you learn to group the beats and develop a sense for when the chords should change.

Because it may take you a while to learn all of the accompaniment patterns, rather than learning all of the patterns at one time, you may want to learn only the strum patterns and use them as you apply the information from the earlier section of the book. Then, as you learn more about playing by ear, keep referring to the sections at the back of the book to learn new accompaniment styles.

Notation

ALTHOUGH THE INFORMATION in this book deals with playing guitar by ear rather than reading music, a knowledge of some basic music notation will be helpful in playing accompaniment styles and learning the rhythms of songs. Some music terms and notation are shown below.

STAFF: the five lines and four spaces
BAR LINE: the vertical lines on the staff
MEASURE: the distance between the bar lines
BEAT: the pulse of the music
TIME SIGNATURE: the fraction which appears at the beginning of the music.
　　　　　　　The top numeral indicates how many beats are in a measure,
　　　　　　　and bottom numeral indicates what type of note will get one beat.
　　　　　　　(e.g., 4 = quarter note will get one beat).

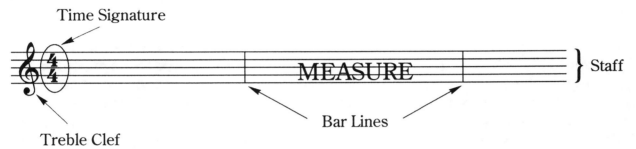

Chord Diagrams

The chords in this book are shown with diagrams such as the one drawn below. On the diagrams, the vertical lines represent the strings with the first string on the right. The horizontal lines represent the frets with the first fret at the top. The dots on or next to the lines indicate where to put left-hand fingers. The numbers on the dots indicate which left-hand finger to use. A zero above the diagram indicates that string under the zero is to be played open. An open string is one that is played without a left-hand finger pushing on it. An X above a string indicates that the string is not to be played.

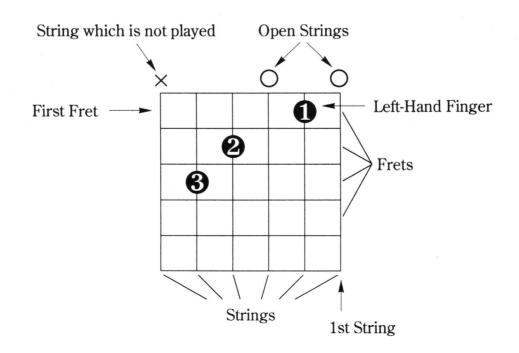

Basic Chords

*THE FOLLOWING DIAGRAMS show basic chords which you should know in order to play the exercises in this book as well as songs you'll be playing by ear. Practice strumming these chords and changing from one chord to another. The order doesn't matter. Try to change the chords so that there is no pause when you change from one to the next. If you already know some of these chords, practice the ones which are new to you.

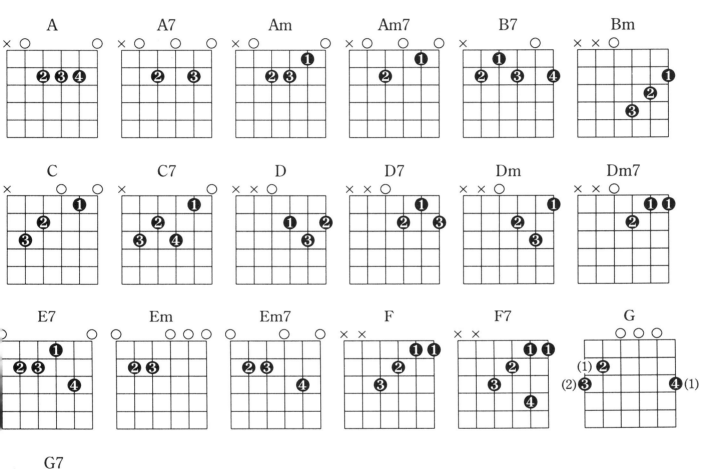

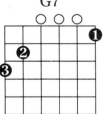

*A more complete collection of chords is given on the *Chord Reference Sheets* in the back of the book.

Finding the Meter of a Song

THE WORD *meter* refers to how many beats there are in a measure. The word *beat* means the pulse of the music. Because you are trying to learn to play by ear, you are not concerned with the measures (remember that in playing by ear you are not using any written music.) But you should be aware of the pulse of the music. If you can determine if the song is in 4/4, 3/4 or 6/8, then you will know which accompaniment pattern (strumming or fingerpicking) to use for the song. If you don't know any accompaniment styles, you should refer to the sections in this book on "Strumming," "Pick-Strum Style" and "Fingerpicking." Until you have learned these accompaniment patterns, you may want to use only down strums to accompany the songs you will be learning to play by ear.

By knowing the meter and *using a strum, pick-strum or fingerpick pattern which will work for that meter,* the song will have a good solid rhythm to it and will help the singer (or singers) to keep "in time" and be together with the accompaniment. Knowing the meter of the song is also helpful in knowing when the chords feel like they should change.

To find the meter or the time of the song, you must first find where the pulse or the beats are in the song. Then, listen for where the accent or the heavy beat falls when you are singing the song. The following example will help you learn to do this. The lyrics to "Down In The Valley" are written below. Sing the words and place a slash above, or between, the words where you think the beat occurs. Next, place an accent mark (>) above the beats that you feel should be heavy or accented. It may be helpful for you to conduct the song (if you know the beat pattern) to find the accent.

1. **Down in the val - ley, valley so low.**

Hang your head o - - ver. Hear the wind blow.

If it felt like the accent to "Down In The Valley" happened every three beats, then you are correct. This song is in 3/4 time. The example below shows the lyrics to "Down In The Valley" with the slashes written where the beats occur and the accent marks written above the accented beats.

```
    >           >   >   >         >
    /     / / / / / / / / /   /   / / /
```
2. **Down in the val - ley, valley so low.**
```
    >               >   >   >             >
    /     /     /   / / / / / / /     /   /   / / /
```
Hang your head o - - ver. Hear the wind blow.

Written below are the lyrics and the chords to "Down In The Valley." A slash has been placed over the words showing where the pulse, or beat, falls with the lyrics. An accent mark has been placed over the beats which would be accented. Practice strumming the chords to this song using only the down strokes. Strum the chords once for each slash that is written. Place an accent on the first of every three strums. If a chord name is not written above a slash, keep strumming the chord that was written last.

Down In The Valley

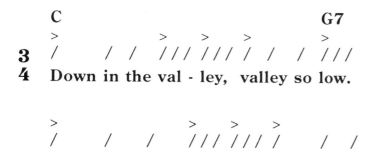

In the next example, "Down In The Valley" has been written out as a *rhythm sheet*. This means that only the lyrics and the chords have been given. The chords are written every three beats. Strum each chord name down three times (one time on each beat). After you have done this, use any of the accompaniment patterns for 3/4 to play "Down In The Valley." Each accompaniment pattern would be played one time for each time a chord name is written. Although measures are not written in the example below, every time a chord name is written it is equal to one measure.

4.

Down In The Valley

```
              >
         C (/   /  /)  C     C     C        G7
  3   1. Down in the val - ley,  valley so low.
  4   2. Build me a  cast - le   forty feet high.
      3. Write me a  let - ter   send it by mail.

         G7              G7  G7  G7          C
      1. Hang your head o - - ver.  Hear the wind blow.
      2. So    I    can see him   as   he  rides by.
      3. Send it    in   care of  Bir-ming-ham jail.
```

Before you go on, try finding the accented beats to "Jingle Bells." The words are written below. Put slashes above the words where the beats would occur. Next, put accent marks above those beats which would be accented. If a beat comes between two words, write a slash between them. See if the accent (the pulse of the music) comes every three beats, or every other beat. If the accent is every other beat, then the song is probably in 4/4. Remember, we are only trying to find where the beats are in the song, not the chords. That will come later.

5.   Jingle Bells

Dashing through the snow, in a one horse open sleigh.

O'er the fields we go, laughing all the way.

Bells on bobtails ring. Making spirits bright.

What fun it is to laugh and sing a sleighing song tonight.

Jingle bells   jingle bells,   jingle all the way.

Oh, what fun it is to ride in a one-horse open sleigh.

Jingle bells   jingle bells,   jingle all the way.

Oh, what fun it is to ride in a one-horse open sleigh.

"Jingle Bells" is in 4/4. The accented beat comes on every other beat. Any of the strum patterns, pick-strum patterns or fingerpicking patterns for 4/4 which are found in the appendix of this book will work to accompany "Jingle Bells."

"Jingle Bells" is written below with the chords. The chord names are written every four beats. First, strum each chord name down four times (one time for each beat). Accent beats two and four. Next, use any of the accompaniment patterns for 4/4. Remember, each time a chord name is written equals one measure (four beats).

6.   **Jingle Bells**

$\frac{4}{4}$ G / /   /   /   G   G   C
Dashing through the snow, in a one horse open sleigh.

C   D   D   G
O'er the fields we go, laughing all the way.

G   G   G   C
Bells on bobtails ring. Making spirits bright.

          C   ·   D   D7   G
What fun it is to laugh and sing a sleighing song to - night.

G   G   G   G
Jingle bells,   jingle bells,   jingle all the way.

C   G   A7   D
Oh, what fun it is to ride in a one-horse open sleigh.

G   G   G   G
Jingle bells,   jingle bells,   jingle all the way.

C   G   D7   G
Oh, what fun it is to ride in a one-horse open sleigh.

Try doing this process on "Amazing Grace" which is written below. Write a slash above or between the words where you think the beats occur. Then, write accent marks above the accented beats. Again, we are only trying to find the beats in the song, not the chords. Sections later in this book will help you find the chords.

7.   **Amazing Grace**

Amazing Grace, How sweet the sound that saved a wretch like me.

I once was lost, but now I'm found, was blind but now I see.

    If you wrote the accented beats to "Amazing Grace" every three beats, you were correct. This song is in 3/4 time.

    The lyrics and the chords to "Amazing Grace" are written below. Because this song is in 3/4 time, you can strum each chord three times or use any of the accompaniment patterns for 3/4 found in the appendix of this book. Accent the first of each three beats.

Notice there is not a chord above "A." The accented strum comes on "maz." This song starts with an imcomplete measure called a "pick-up beat." You can strum the first chord (E) one time for the pick-up.

8.   **Amazing Grace**

    The next steps in playing by ear are to find the key, the beginning pitch to sing, and the chords to the song. The following sections of the book will help you learn to do these.

Finding the First Chord of the Song

FINDING THE FIRST chord to the song is one of the most important steps in playing by ear. This chord is invaluable to finding the key and the rest of the chords to the song. If you have a melody and you want to put chords to it, as in a sing-a-long or sing-around-the-campfire situation, you can begin by strumming any chord and singing the melody. Of course, the melody note must be the right one for the chord. Also, in selecting the first chord, if the melody is melancholy or sad, the first chord will probably be a minor chord. If the melody has a lighter or happier feel, the first chord will probably be major. Make sure that the first chord is one you can play easily. The first chord will often (but not always) be the key. The easiest keys in order of difficulty are: G, C, D, A, E and F. The easiest minor keys in order of difficulty are Em, Am, Dm and Bm. Try starting with one of these chords first. While playing the first chord, try singing the melody beginning on the pitch which is the same as one of the strings in the chord you are holding. Sing the melody. If it sounds right, you've started on the correct pitch. If it sounds off, try singing the melody beginning on the pitch of one of the other strings in the chord. Either you will be right on target or so far off that you won't be able to stand it. Now that you have found the first note of the melody and the first chord of the song, and you know the meter of the song, the next step is to find the rest of the chords to the song. You will learn how to do this in later sections of this book.

Before you go on, practice holding a simple chord and find the beginning pitch to each of the following familiar tunes.

"Amazing Grace"
"Home On The Range"
"My Bonnie Lies Over The Ocean"

The following song has only one chord in the entire song. Practice holding any chord and find the beginning pitch. Keep strumming the chord down and sing the song. If some of the other sections of this book get a bit frustrating, you can keep coming back to this song as an ego builder.

9.

Are You Sleeping

```
       G              G              G           G
 4   / / / /      / / / /        / / / /    / / / /
 4   Are you sleeping? Are you sleeping, brother John, brother John?

     G              G
     /     / / /    /     / /
     How are you today, sir? Very fine, I thank you.

     G            G
     / /  / / /   /    / /
     Ding, dong, ding. Ding, dong, ding.
```

If you are trying to take a song off of a record (transcribing), listen to the bass player to get the first chord. Very often the first rule of bass playing is to play the root (the note which has the same letter name as the chord) on the first beat. Listen to the first note the bass player plays and try to match that pitch on the low strings of your guitar. When you find the note, think of which chord has that note in the bottom of it. If the bass note matches but the chord sounds wrong, try the minor version of that chord, or the seventh version of that chord *(e.g., G7 rather than G).*

If you have the tape which accompanies this book, listen to the following examples and by matching the bass notes determine the chords.

10.   Tape

11.   Tape

12.   Tape

Chords in the Major Keys

AFTER YOU HAVE found the first chord to the song, you now have to find the rest of the chords. In order to do this you have to know which chords go together or sound good together. Generally, chords which sound good together are in the same key. For our purposes, the *key* is the pitch or the chord to which the other chords or notes want to return. For example, play a G chord, the C, Am, then D7 and stop. Hear how the D7 wants to go to G. In this case, G is the key and the other chords in the key (*i.e.,* C, Am and D7) want to return to it.

The following illustration is a chord clock. It is sometimes called a *circle of fifths*. Knowing how to use this clock will be one of the most important concepts you can learn from this book. The chord clock will show you how to find the key of a song, how to find the chords which go together in each key, and how to transpose (change the key) of a song.

THE CHORD CLOCK (*Circle of Fifths*)

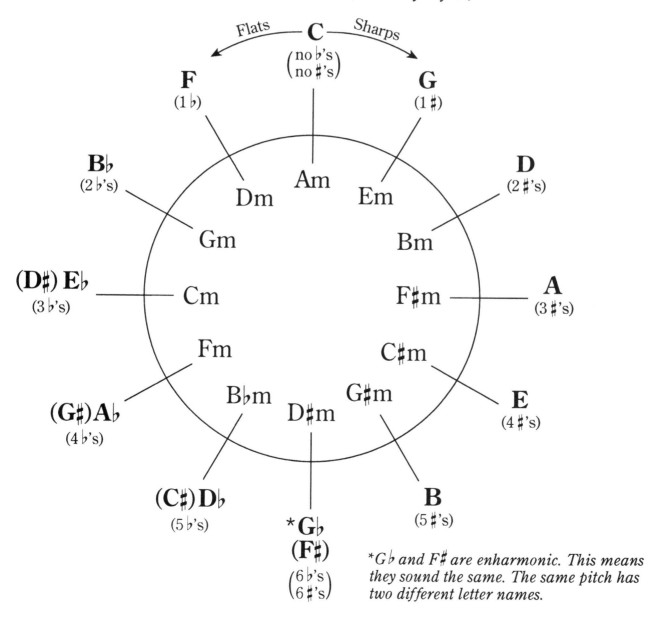

G♭ and F♯ are enharmonic. This means they sound the same. The same pitch has two different letter names.

Although this book deals with playing by ear (which means you have no written music), you may have some music which has the melody and lyrics but no guitar chords. Even though you have the music, you are still playing by ear because you have to find the chords. The chord clock will help you find those chords. You can find the key and the chords by using the clock. To find the key of the song, look at the key signature. The *key signature* is the sharps or flats written at the beginning of the music before the fraction called the *time signature*. The number of sharps or flats in the key signature will tell you the key in which the song is written. If the song has no sharps or flats at the beginning in the key signature, then the song is in the key of C (or Am). On the clock C is at the top. If the song has one or more sharps in the key signature, it will be in one of the keys on the right half of the chord clock. As you move from C to the right, each key will have one more sharp in the key signature. For example, the key of G (or Em) will have one sharp in the key signature. The key of D (Bm) will have two sharps. The key of A (F#m) will have three sharps, and so on. If a song has one or more flats in its key signature, it will be in one of the keys on the left half of the clock. Each key to the left of C will have one more flat added to its key signature. For example, the key of F (Dm) will have one flat, B♭ (Gm) will have two flats, E♭ (Cm) will have three flats, and so on. By knowing what key the song is in, you can find all of the chords to the song. Several key signatures are written below. In the blanks above the key signature write the names of the keys. The first two have been filled in.

13.

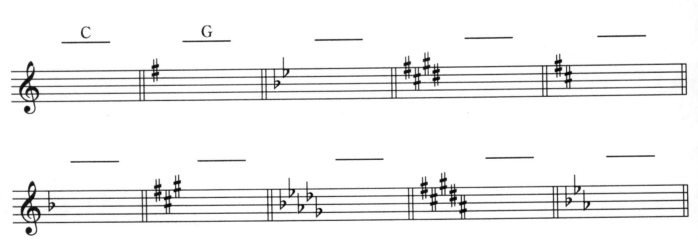

Finding the Chords to Songs in Major Keys

WHETHER YOU HAVE the written music or not, you can determine the six basic chords in any given key by using the chord clock. Major and minor chords are found on the chord clock. Major chords are those which have only a letter name. Major chords may also be sharp or flat. Minor chords have an "m" written by them and generally sound more sad or melancholy than do major chords.

To find the basic chords in a key, take the chord having the name of the key (key chord) and the first two chords clockwise and counterclockwise of the key chord. Those three chords and their related chords (chords on the inside of the clock which are connected and correspond to the three outside chords) make up the six basic chords in any given key. For example: to find the chords in the key of G, find G on the chord clock. Locate the chords clockwise and counterclockwise of G (C and D). Now find the related chords to G, C and D (Em, Am and Bm). You now have found the six basic chords in the key of G which are G, C, D, Em, Am and Bm. This will work for every key. Knowing this process is invaluable to the person who wants to play by ear. It's also helpful in writing your own songs. On the clock below, the chords in the key of E have also been circled. Notice that the easiest keys for the guitar are G, C, D, A, E and F, in that order. **In a major key, the most commonly used chords are those on the outside of the clock.** These are sometimes called the *primary chords*. For example, the primary chords in the key of G would be G, C and D. If you are trying to find the chords to a song by ear, try the primary chords in the key first. If they don't work, try the chords in the key which are on the inside of the clock.

An excellent way to train your ear to hear chord changes is to write your own progressions. A *chord progression* is a series of chords. In the blanks above the measures below, write chords from the key in any order. If you don't like the sound of a particular chord you have chosen, try another chord from the key until you get the progression sounding the way you would like. You can use the same chord more than once, let the same chord get more than one measure, and put two chords in a measure if you would like. Don't be afraid to experiment. The key signature and the first chord and last chords have been given in each progression. The first and last chords have the same name as the key in which you will be playing. Not all songs begin and end with the key chord, but at first it would be a good idea to write progressions which do. Fill in the blanks with chords from the key. Practice strumming or fingerpicking your progressions.

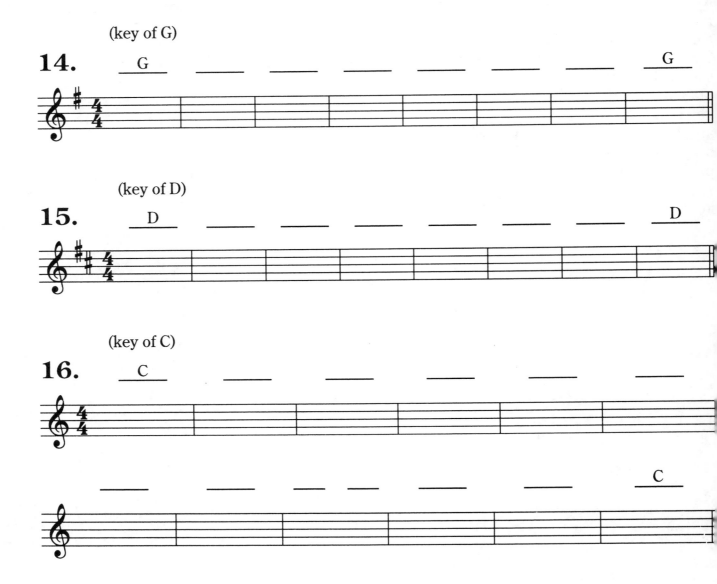

The music to "Silent Night" is written below. The melody, lyrics, measures, time signature and key signature are written. Because there is one sharp, this song is in the key of G. The first chord (key chord) has been written above the first measure. Some of the other measures have blanks above them. The blanks show where the chord changes come. Using the chords in the key of G, fill in the blanks with the correct chords. You may have to try several chords from the key of G until you find the correct one. Sometimes more than one chord will work in one place.

17.

If you don't have the music, you can still use the information from the clock to play by ear. Suppose you want to play "She'll Be Comin' Round The Mountain" without the use of music. Choose the key you want to use (make it an easy one) and then strum (or fingerpick) the key chord and sing the melody. Remember, most simple sing-a-long songs begin and end with the key chord. Use the information you learn from the section in this book on "Finding the First Chord to the Song" to find which note you should begin singing. When it sounds like the melody you are singing clashes with the chord you are playing, try one of the other chords from the key. You may have to try several until you find the correct one. Finding the right chords is a process of trial and error. As your ear develops, the errors will be fewer. Eventually, there will be none. The trick is to train your ear to hear the correct chord before you play it. With practice, this will start to happen. First, try using the chords on the outside of the clock. These are the primary chords and are used most often. If the chords on the outside of the clock do not work, try using the chords from the key which are on the inside of the clock. Traditional campfire-type songs are some of the best tunes to begin learning to play by ear.

The following song has only two chords in it. Above the lyrics below, fill in the blanks with the correct chords. The first chord is given.

18.   He's Got The Whole World

$\frac{4}{4}$
                       __G__
He's got the whole world in his hands.

                       _____
He's got the whole world in his hands.

                       _____
He's got the whole world in his hands.

                       _____   ____
He's got the whole world in his hands.

Above the following lyrics write the correct chords. No blanks are given to fill in. You determine the key and where the chord changes should happen.

19.   She'll Be Comin' Round The Mountain

She'll be com-in' round the mountain when she comes, She'll be

com-in' round the moun-tain when she comes, She'll be com-in'

round the moun-tain, she'll be com-in' round the moun-tain,

she'll be com-in' round the moun-tain when she comes.

After you know where the chords change, and what chords they will be, find the meter (time) of the song and use accompaniment patterns that will work for 4/4, 3/4 or 6/8 to play the song.

Written below are the lyrics to "Michael Row The Boat Ashore." First, find the meter (timing) of the song to know which accompaniment pattern to use. If you don't know some accompaniment patterns to use, you can use down strums and play the chords to the song. Next, select a key and while playing the key chord, find the beginning pitch of the song. Finally, find the other chords to the song by singing the melody and when it sounds like the melody clashes with the chord you are playing, try one of the other chords from the key until you find the correct one. **Congratulations!!! You are playing by ear.**

20.   Michael Row The Boat Ashore

?   Mich - ael   row   the   boat   a - shore,   Al - le - lu - ia.

Mich - ael   row   the   boat   a - shore,   Al - le - lu - ia.

Chords in the Minor Keys

THE METHOD USED for finding the chords in minor keys is similar to the method for finding chords in major keys. Again, the chord clock is used. To find the chords in a minor key, find the minor chord on the clock which has the name of the key you want to work with. To find the chords in that key, take the chords clockwise and counterclockwise of the key chord (chord which has the letter name of the key) and the chords connected to them on the outside of the clock. Next, change the name of the chord clockwise of the key from a minor chord to a 7th chord. You now have found the six basic chords in that minor key. For example, the six basic chords in the key of Am are: Am, Dm, E7, C, F and G. On the chord clock below, the chords for the key of Am have been circled.

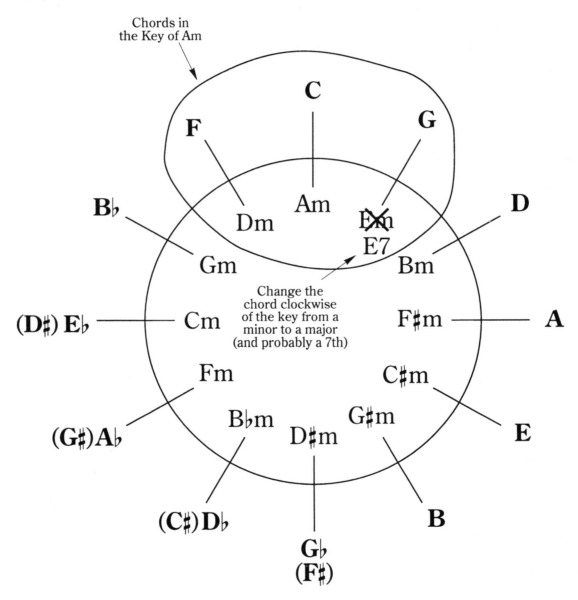

In a minor key, the most frequently used chords are the ones on the inside of the clock. For example, in the key of Am, the most often used chords would be: Am, Dm and E7. If you are trying to find the chords to a song by ear and the song is in a minor key, try the chords from the key which are on the inside of the clock first. If they don't work, try the chords in the key which are on the outside of the clock.

Again, an excellent way to train your ear is to write your own chord progressions. Try writing several of your own progressions in the examples below. Fill in the blanks with chords from the minor key. The key chord is written in the first and last blanks.

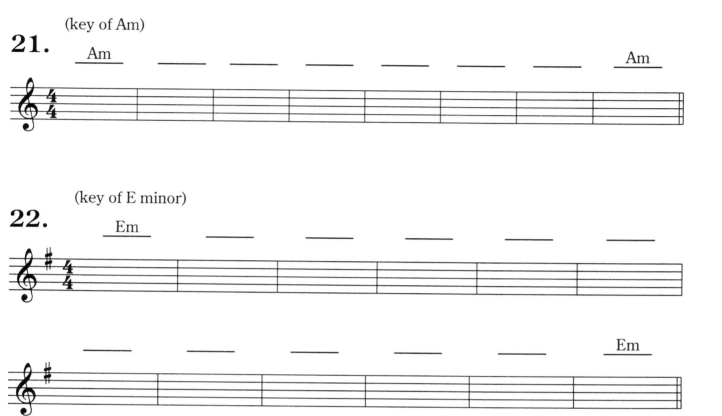

21. (key of Am)

Am   Am

22. (key of E minor)

Em

Em

Finding the Chords to Songs in Minor Keys

USING THE SAME process you did to find the chords to a song in a major key, find the chords to the following songs in minor keys. First, find the meter of the song. Next, play the key chord of your choice and find the beginning pitch for the melody. Then, sing the song and find the other chords. Use the chord clock to find the chords in the minor key which you have selected. Strum down or apply strumming or fingerpicking patterns from the accompaniment sections of this book. Find the chords to the following song in minor key. The melody has been given in case you don't know the tune. Blanks have been written above the measures where the chords change. Using the chords from the key of Em, fill in the blanks with the correct chords.

23.   A Poor Wayfaring Stranger

Find the chords to the following song in a minor key. Write the chords above the lyrics. Begin with an easy minor chord. You'll notice on the clock that the easiest minor keys for the guitar are: Am, Em and Dm. After selecting the first chord, sing the melody and when the melody clashes with the chord, try another chord from the minor key. A star is written where a chord is used in this song which is not in the key. To find this chord, try one of the chords which are close on the clock to the chords in the key.

24.   Scarborough Fair

?   Are you go-ing to Scar-bor-ough Fair?

                            ★
       Par-sley, sage, rose-ma-ry and thyme.

       Re-mem-ber me to one who lives there,

       She once was a true love of mine.

Barre Chords

A "BARRE CHORD" is a chord which has a finger (usually the first finger) lying, or barring, across some or all of the strings. Knowing how barre chords work will enable you to play the chords in any key, especially those keys that contain chords which are sharp or flat. Knowing how to play barre chords will also help you to play more complex chords rather than just the basic major and minor chords. Although any chord can be played as a barre chord, you will want to use them primarily on the chords which have a sharp or flat in the name of the chord. In this book you will be shown two categories of barre chords: those which have the roots on the sixth string and those which have roots on the fifth string. Knowing the barre chord patterns will make it possible for you to play hundreds of chords.

> **Because the material in this section of the book may be more difficult to play than the other sections, you may want to practice only a portion of it and then move ahead. Then, keep coming back until you have the barre chords mastered.**

First Category

THE FOLLOWING DIAGRAMS show barre chord patterns from the first category. These chords have their roots (note which names the chord) on the sixth string. All six strings can be strummed or fingerpicked with these chords. In the chart above the diagrams, the numbers show in which fret to place the barre finger. The letters show what the letter name of the chord will be when the bar finger is placed in that fret. The diagrams show the fingerings for the various types of chords (*i.e.*, minor, 7th, etc.). Major chords are those which have only letter names (A, D, F, etc.). Major chords may also be sharp or flat.

Sixth String Roots

1	3	5	7	8	10	12	Fret
F	G	A	B	C	D	E	Root (chord letter name)

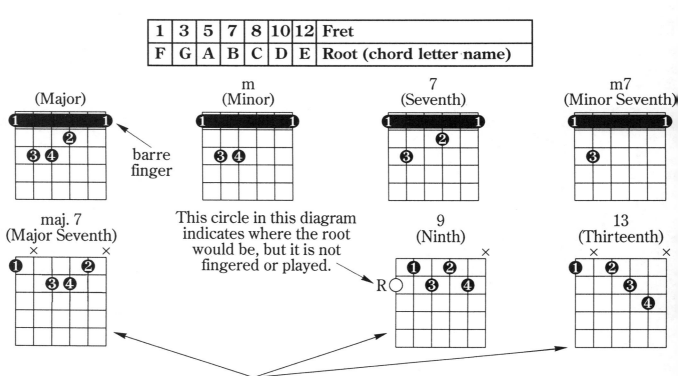

These chord patterns do not have a bar finger. The root is still on the sixth string. The "x" above a string indicates a finger should be tilted and lightly touch that string so it doesn't sound when strummed.

24

To find a barre chord using the chart and the diagrams, do the following: First, place the barre finger in the fret number which corresponds to the root name (letter name) of the chord you're trying to play (A7 would have the barre finger in the fifth fret because the root for A is in the fifth fret, on the sixth string); then, hold the pattern for the type of chord you want to play (major, minor, 7th, etc.). To sharp a barre chord, move the entire pattern up one fret. To flat a barre chord, move the pattern down one fret.

G♯m7 would be played like the diagram below. G♯m7 is in the fourth fret because the root for G♯ is in the fourth fret. The fingering for a minor seventh chord is used.

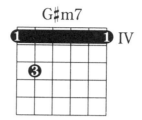

Practice the following progressions using barre chords only **from the first category.** In actual playing, many of these chords would not be played as barre chords, but to help you learn barre chords, play all of these chords as barre chords. First, strum down four times in each measure. Then, use strumming or fingerpicking accompaniment patterns which can be found in the appendix of this book.

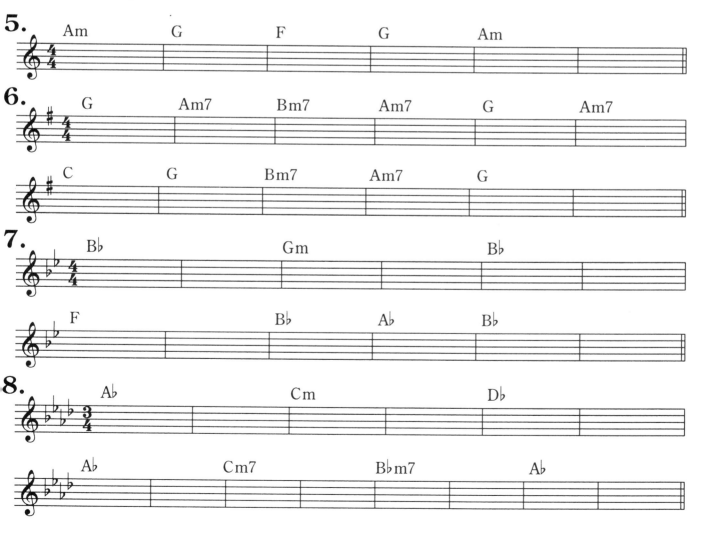

Second Category

BY KNOWING TWO categories of barre chords, chord changes may be kept close amd more convenient. Also, many times only one or two chords in a song will be played as barre chords. The other chords will be open chords. By knowing two categories of barre chords, the barre chord can be played in frets close to the open chords.

The second category of barre chords has the root on the fifth string. Although all of the strings may be strummed, these chords may sound better if only five strings are strummed or fingerpicked. In the chart above the diagrams, the numbers show in which fret on the fifth string to place the bar finger. The letters show what the letter name (root) of the chord will be when the bar finger is placed in that fret. As with the first category of barre chords, to sharp a barre chord, move the entire pattern up one fret and to flat a barre chord, move the pattern down one fret. The diagrams show the fingerings for the various types of chords. Because the root for D would be in the fifth fret, the D7 chord would be played like this:

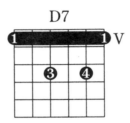

Because the root is on the fifth string, the second category of barre chords will generally sound best if only five strings are strummed.

Fifth String Roots

2	3	5	7	8	10	12	Fret
B	C	D	E	F	G	A	Root (chord letter name)

An "x" above the string in these diagrams means that string is not played.

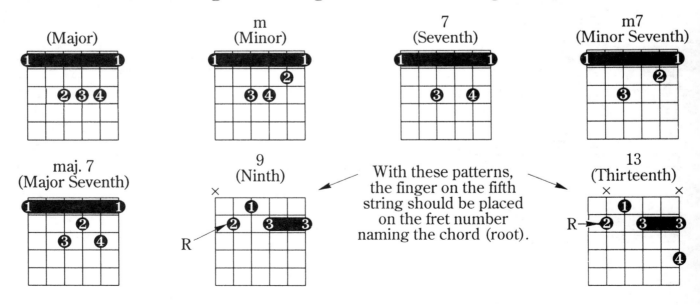

With these patterns, the finger on the fifth string should be placed on the fret number naming the chord (root).

The same process is used in finding these chords as was used in finding the position and fingering for the barre chords with the roots on the sixth string. For example, if you wanted to find a C♯m7 chord, place the barre finger on the fourth fret because the C♯ root is on the fifth string, fourth fret (C is in the third fret and to sharp it you move it up one fret), then hold the pattern for a m7 chord. So, a C♯m7 chord would be played like this:

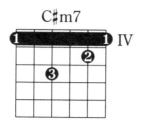

If you use pick-strum or fingerpicking accompaniment patterns with barre chords from the second category, play them as five-string chords.

Practice the following progressions using **only barre chords from the second category.** Play all of the chords in these progressions as barre chords.

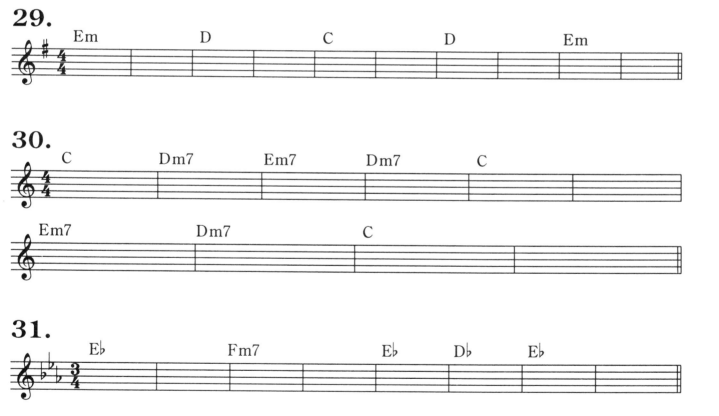

Knowing two categories of barre chords will make your chord changes more convenient. For example, if you are playing an F♯m and the next chord is Bm, it would be best to play F♯m in the second fret using the first category of barre chords, and then play Bm in the second fret using the second category as drawn below. Otherwise, Bm would be in the seventh fret using the first category. Going from the second fret to the seventh fret is not nearly as easy as staying in the second fret.

Practice the following progressions using barre chords from both categories. You may have to figure out both ways of playing a barre chord and then use the one which is closest to the chord you just played. Play all of the chords in these progressions as barre chords.

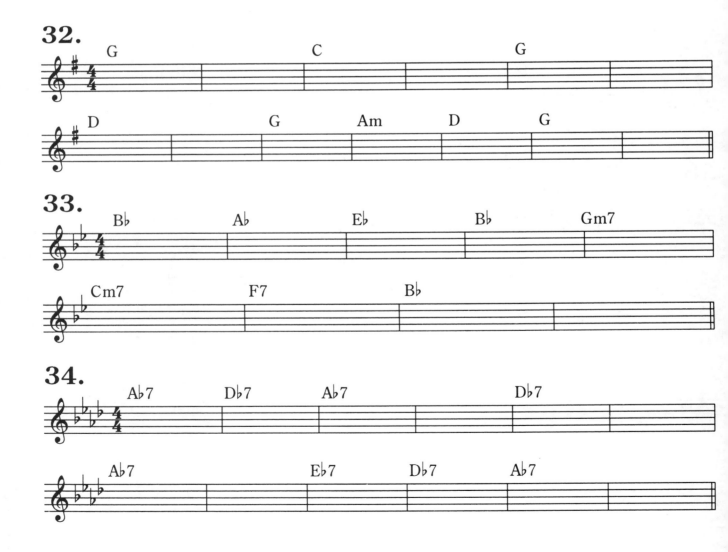

35.

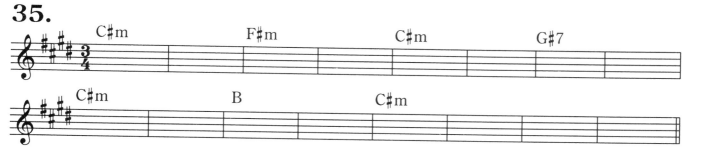

In "real life" actual playing, it would be rare that all of the chords to a song would be played as barre chords especially if you are playing acoustic guitar. If you have a choice of playing Am as an open chord or as a barre chord, go for the open chord. Again, a good que that a chord is to be played as a barre chord is the presence of a sharp or flat sign. In the following progressions, the circled chords should be played a barre chords. The chords which are not circled should be played as open chords. Practice the progressions first using only down strums, then use strum or fingerpick accompaniment patterns. Practice changing smoothly from the open chords to the barre chords.

36.

37.

38.

39.

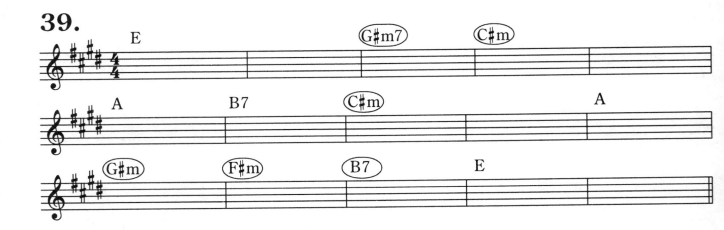

Knowing barre chords will be helpful in playing songs by ear because you may wish to play the songs in keys which contain barre chords. If you look back at the chord clock, you will see that keys which contain more sharps or flats also have more chords which need to be played as barre chords. Write some of your own original chord progressions in keys which contain barre chords. Use the chord clock to find which chords go together in the different keys.

Chord Embellishment

"CHORD EMBELLISHMENT" REFERS to "spicing up" the basic major and/or minor chords by adding more notes to make the chords richer and give them more color. For example, G7 has a more colorful sound than does a plain G chord. The information in this section of the book will show you what can be added to the basic chords in the key to make the chords sound more colorful. If you are playing by ear this will help because you may have found the chord which sounds "almost correct" for a certain part of the song but is not quite right. By knowing what can be added to the chords, you can zero in on the exact chord to be used.

The first step in embellishment chords is to arrange all of the chords in a given key in alphabetical order. First, find the chords in a given key. **Use the chord clock** from the earlier section in this book to help you find all of the basic chords in a given key. For example, the chords in the key of C are C, F, G, Dm, Am and Em. Next, begin with the chord which has the same letter name as the key, and arrange the chords in a key in alphabetical order. For example, the chords in the key of C arranged in alphabetical order would be C, Dm, Em, F, G and Am. Remember, in the musical alphabet A follows G. Practice arranging in alphabetical order the chords in the keys of G, D, A, E and F. Be sure to begin with the chord name which has the same letter name as the key. Next, once you have arranged the chords of the key in alphbetical order, assign each of the chords in the key a Roman numeral. The key chord (the chord which has the same letter name as the key) will be assigned the Roman numeral I. The second chord in the key (in alphabetical order) is the ii chord. The third chord in the key is iii, then IV, V, and vi. The following chart shows the chords in the key of D under the Roman numerals used to identify the chords.

I	ii	iii	IV	V	vi
D	Em	F♯m	G	A	Bm

The large Roman numerals are used on the I, IV and V chords because they are major chords. In every major key the I, IV and V chords are major. The small Roman numerals are used for the minor chords. In every major key ii, iii and vi chords are minor. Memorize the chords in the common keys of C, G, D, A, E and E. These are very popular keys for guitar. You could also figure out the six basic chords in each key by writing out the major scale of that key and then thinking of the Roman numeral order and which of the chords are major and which are minor. For example, if I wanted to find the chords in the key of A, I would write out the names of the notes in the A scale which are: A, B, C♯, D, E, F♯ and G♯. Next, I would take the Roman numeral sequence (I, ii, iii, IV and vi) and match the notes of the A scale with the Roman numerals.

I	ii	iii	IV	V	vi	VII
A	B	C♯	D	E	F♯	G♯

Next, make the chords under the small Roman numerals minor.

I	ii	iii	IV	V	vi	VII
A	Bm	C♯m	D	E	F♯m	G♯dim

Notice that the VII chord is diminished. This chord does not appear on the chord clock. It is an uncommon chord to use in sing-a-long, or campfire-type songs, but it would be good for you to know that it is in the key.

Now that you have assigned the basic chords in the key a Roman numeral, the chart below shows what embellishments can be added to the chords in the key. For example, in the key of C the IV chord is F. So, in the key of C you can play Fmaj7, F6, Fadd9, or any of the other embellishments for the IV chord. If you are playing a song in the key of C, and using the F chord sounds almost right in a certain place in the song, try playing the embellishments of the F chord until you find the correct one. Eventually, you should train your ear to hear the correct embellishment being used.

If you do not know the fingering for a certain type of embellished chord, refer to the Chord Reference Section in the Appendix of this book or the section on Barre Chords.

I, IV	Major, 6th, maj. 7, add 9, maj. 9, sus.
V	Major, 7th, 7sus., 9th, 11th, 13th
ii	minor, m7, m7sus., m9, m6, m7-5
iii, vi	minor, m7, m7sus., m9

One of the most frequently used embellishments is to play the V chord as a 7th chord. For example, in the key of G, it would be very common to use a D7 chord rather than a D chord.

Knowing how to embellish chords is also invaluable in writing your own chord progressions. Practice writing chord progressions in several keys using the basic chords and then go back and embellish the progression.

The following two examples show how embellishments can be added to a chord progression. In the first example, a basic chord progression has been written in the key of C. The Roman numerals for the chords in the key of C have been written in parentheses next to the chord names.

40.

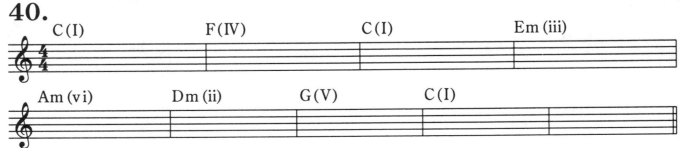

32

The next example shows the same progression with embellishments added. Practice strumming this example. If you don't know some of the chords, refer to the Chord Reference Section in the Appendix of this book or the section on Barre Chords. Notice how the chords sound more rich and colorful with the embellishments added.

41.

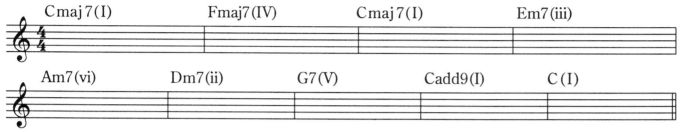

In the following song, find the chord which could be a 7th chord. Don't be afraid to experiment and play several of the chords as 7th chords. Some will sound bad, and others will work.

42.

Silent Night

Where the D chords appeared, if you played D7 rather than D, you were correct. Because D is the V chord in the key of G, and the V in any key can be a 7th chord, D7 works well in "Silent Night."

The following progression is in the key of D. The Roman numerals have been placed next to the chord names showing which chord they are in the key. Using the rules of chord embellishment, add embellishments to the chords. Be careful not to add embellishments which are too difficult for you to play. You may want to begin by adding only 7, m7 or maj7 to the chords. Practice strumming or fingerpicking the following progression.

43.

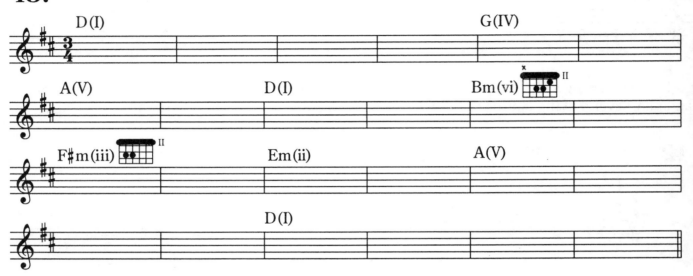

The next example shows some embellishments which could have been added to the previous song. Your version of this song could have been, and probably was, different. The possible ways of embellishing a song are almost limitless.

44.

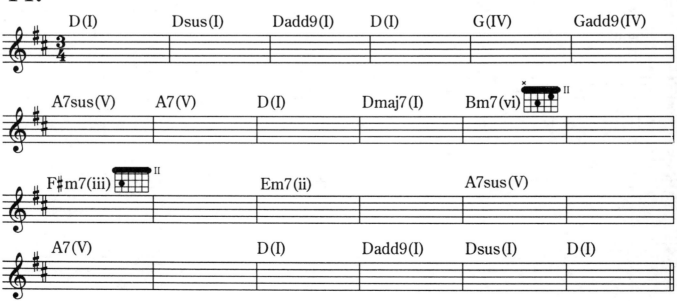

Common Chord Progressions

NOW THAT YOU know which Roman numerals are assigned to the chords in a key, it may be helpful to know some common chord progressions. A *progression* is a series of chords. Written below are some common progressions. For example, the V chord often goes to the I chord. The chords in a key won't always be played in the order shown below, but these progressions happen frequently enough that you should be aware of them. Because the progressions are written with Roman numerals, they can be applied to any key. Written in parentheses next to each Roman numeral is what the name of the chord would be in the key of G. Train your ear to hear these progressions. For example, learn what a V chord to a I chord sounds like in any key. This is very helpful when playing by ear. Practice playing these progressions in several keys. Strum each chord as many times as you like.

V(D) $\longrightarrow$ **I(G)**

IV(C) $\longrightarrow$ **V(D)** $\longrightarrow$ **I(G)**

ii(Am) $\longrightarrow$ **V(D)** $\longrightarrow$ **I(G)**

vi(Em) $\longrightarrow$ **ii(Am)** $\longrightarrow$ **V(D)** $\longrightarrow$ **I(G)**

iii(Bm) $\longrightarrow$ **vi(Em)** $\longrightarrow$ **ii(Am)** $\longrightarrow$ **V(D)** $\longrightarrow$ **I(G)**

Extended Chords

IT IS COMMON in a song to use chords other than the six basic chords in a key. The term *extended chords* is used in this book to identify these chords. *Secondary dominants* are one type of extended chords. For the purposes of this book, I won't go into a lengthy description of what a secondary dominant is. Simply put, a secondary dominant is when one of the chords in a key, which was a minor chord, is changed to a major chord (and probably a 7th chord). For example, in the key of G, not only can the G, C, D, Am, Em and Bm chords be used but also A7, E7 and B7 chords can also be used. On the chord clock below, you can see the chords which have been changed into secondary dominants for the key of G. Composers will often use these extended chords to give the music a lift or happy feeling. If you are trying to find the chords to a song, and you have found many of the chords to the song but there is one chord which has got you stumped, change the minor chords in the key to 7th chords and try each of them. One of those chords will probably be the one you are looking for.

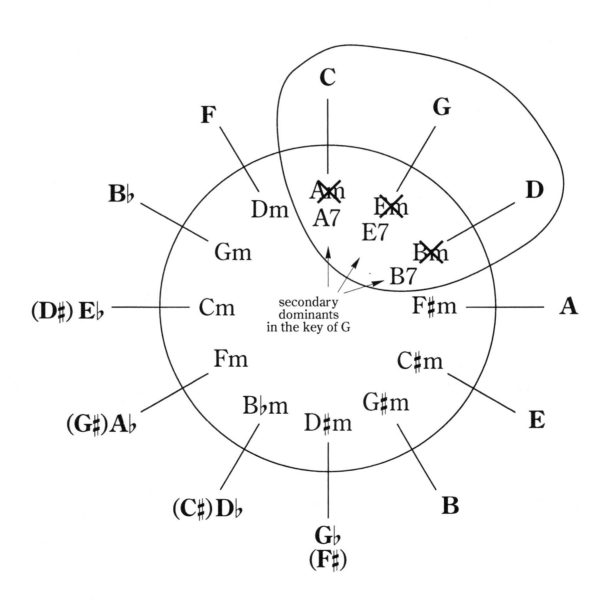

Write several of your own chord progressions using secondary dominants.

In the following songs, the chords are given to you above the lyrics. Secondary dominants are used where the blanks are written. Find the correct secondary dominant chord. The key for each one of these songs is the same as the letter name of the first chord in the song.

45.   My Bonnie Lies Over The Ocean

3   G / / / C   G   G   G   ____   D   D
4   My bonnie lies o-ver the o-cean.   My bonnie lies o-ver the sea.

       G   C   G   G   ____   D   G   G
       My bonnie lies o-ver the o-cean.   Oh, bring back my bonnie to me.

G   G   C   C   D   D   G   G
Bring back, bring back, oh, bring back my bonnie to me, to me.

G   G   C   C   D   D   G
Bring back, bring back, oh, bring back my bonnie to me.

46.   Home On The Range

3   G   G   C   C
4   Oh, give me a home where the buf-fa-lo roam,

       G   ____   D7   D7
       where the deer and the an-te-lope play.

       G   G   C   C
Where seldom is heard a dis-cour-ag-ing word,

       G   D7   G   G
and the skies are not cloudy all day.

G   D7   G   G   G   ____   D7   D7
Home, home on the range.   Where the deer and the an-te-lope play.

       G   G   C   C
Where seldom is heard and dis-cour-aging word,

       G   D7   G
and the skies are not cloudy all day.

Find the chords which go to the following song. Blanks show where the chords change. Three of the chords in this song are secondary dominants. The blanks with stars above them show where the secondary dominants belong.

47.   **It Came Upon A Midnight Clear**

4
4   G   ___ ___ ___ ___   ___   ★___   ___

It came up - on a mid - night clear, That glo - i - ous song of old,

___ ___ ___   ___ ___ ___

From an-gels bend-ing near the earth, To touch their harps of gold.

     ★___   ___   ★___   ___

Peace on the earth, good will to men, From heav'n's all gra-cious King.

___ ___ ___ ___ ___   ___ ___ ___

The world in sol - emn still - ness lay,   To hear the an-gels sing.

Another type of extended chord is the *borrowed chord*. A borrowed chord is a chord which is used (borrowed) from another key. Very often borrowed chords which are used have the same letter name as the major chords in the key, but they have been changed to minor chords. For example, in the key of D, you may see not only the chords in the key (D, G, A, Em, Bm and F♯m), but you may also see Dm, Gm and Am. The Am would be least likely. On the chord clock below, you can see the chords which would be borrowed chords for the key of D.

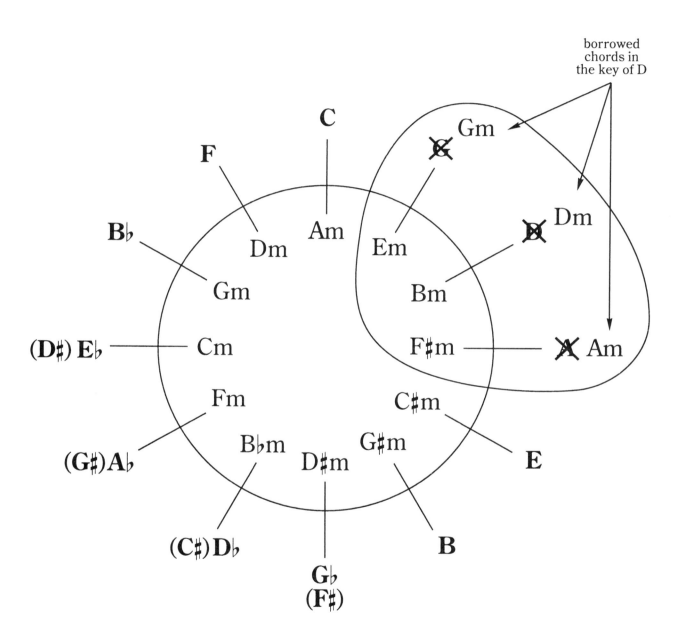

The chords are written above the lyrics to the following song. The blank shows where a borrowed chord is used. Find the borrowed chord. The song is in the key of C.

48.   **When The Saints Go Marching In**

4
4

       G   G   G
  Oh, when the saints go march-ing in,

   G   G   G   D7
  Oh, when the saints go march-ing in.

 D7   G G7   C   ____
  I want to be in their num-ber,

       G   C D7 G
 When the saints go march-ing in.

How to Transpose a Song

TO "TRANSPOSE" A song means to change the key. This may be necessary if the melody is too high or low for you to sing. Another reason for transposing a song could be that the chords may be too difficult for you to play. Transposing the song can make the chords easier. For example, if you have the music to a song which is in the key of B♭ and the chords to the song are B♭, E♭, Cm7 and F7, you could make the chords simpler by transposing the song into an easier key such as G. All of the chords to the song would then be made easier.

The chord clock can be used to transpose a song. To transpose a song, follow the steps written below.

1.   Change the first chord in the piece to one of the simple key chords. Remember, the easiest keys for the guitar in order of difficulty are: G, C, D, A, E and F. The easiest minor keys are: Em, Am, Dm and Bm. You cannot change a major chord to a minor chord and vice versa. However, chords can be simplified. If you are transposing a chord name which sounds difficult to play, such as F13-9, the chord names can be reduced. For example, a Dmaj7 can be reduced to a D chord, Em9 can be reduced to an Em chord, and a G13-9 can be reduced to a G7 chord. To reduce chords you can use the rules of embellishment in reverse. Basically, you are "unembellishing" the chords. Chords which have names larger than 7 can be reduced to 7 chords. The m9 chords can be reduced to m7 chords.

2.   On the chord clock, find the original first chord of the song.

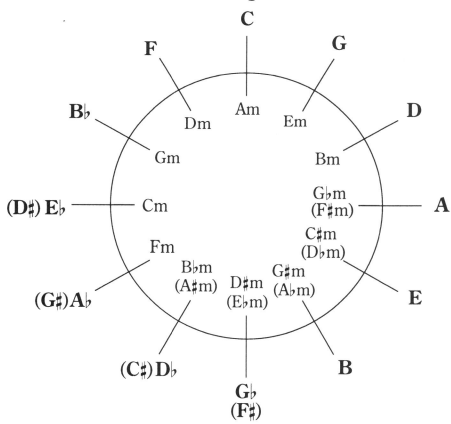

3.   Find your new first chord on the chord clock. This is the new key in which you are playing.

4. **See which direction (clockwise or counterclockwise) and how far (chord names) you moved on the chord clock to change the old original chord to the new chord.**

5. **Change the rest of the chords in the piece the same direction and distance on the chord clock as the first chord was changed.** Major chords change to major chords and minor chords change to minor chords. If a chord in the song is not on the clock, reduce it to a chord name which does appear on the clock.

In example no. 49, the original chord progression was in the key of B♭. The original chords are written on the bottom. The chords have been changed to the key of G. The new chords are written on the top. To change this progression from the key of B♭ to the key of G, the chords all had to be moved clockwise three steps or three moves on the chord clock as shown below. When transposing the Gm7 chord, a Gm was used. The Gm chord then moved to Em. If you want to use Em7 (putting the 7 back on), you can. Or, you can use simply Em. Notice that the F7-5 has been changed to D7.

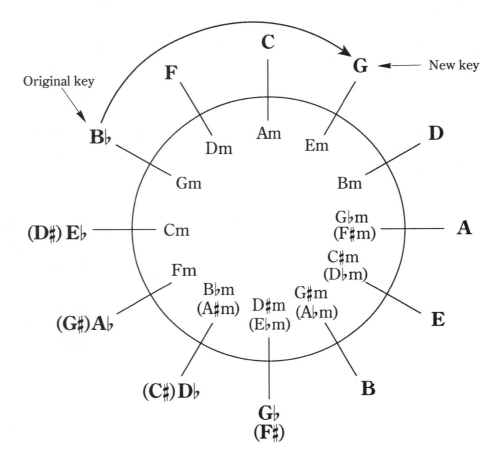

49.

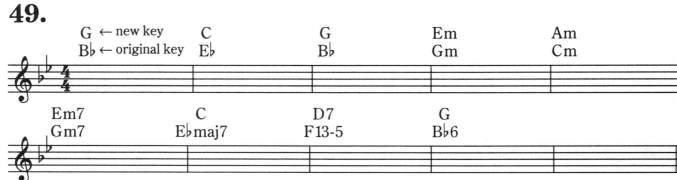

Transpose the following example from the key of E♭ to the key of C. In this case, the chords will be moving clockwise three steps, or three moves. Write the new chords above the old chord names.

50.

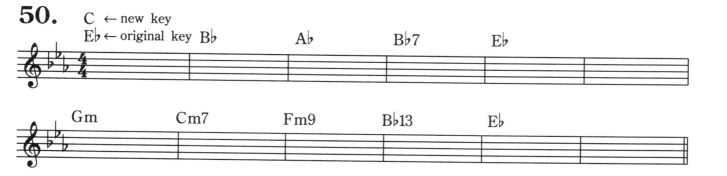

Using the Capo

ANOTHER WAY TO transpose a song is to use a "capo." A capo is a clamp which attaches to the guitar neck. When the capo is placed in a fret, the chords are fingered as though the next fret up the neck from the capo is the first fret. The capo raises the pitch of the chords ½ step for every fret the capo is moved up the neck. With the capo in the second fret, the G chord will sound like an A chord. It's really not necessary that you know the sounding pitch name of the chord unless you are playing guitar and someone else is playing another instrument such as piano and you want to play in the same key. As far as playing by ear is concerned, with the capo on, just think of the chord names as being what the chord looks like rather than the actual pitch it is sounding. With the capo in the fourth fret, try playing a song in the key of G. The pitch of the chords, and the melody, will be higher.

The capo can also be used to make songs sound lower. If a song is too high for you to sing, place the capo up the neck and play the same chords. Now the song may be way too high for you to sing, but you can sing the song an octave lower.

Appendix

Strum Patterns

KNOWING THE POSSIBLE strum patterns, pick-strum patterns, and fingerpicking patterns which can be used will be a great help in accompanying the songs you will be playing by ear. This section of the book will show you strum patterns which can be used to accompany the songs in this book and other songs you will be playing by ear. Not only will they be helpful in playing songs by ear, but they could be used in your own original songs or songs from sheet music or songbooks. This section of the book will show you many different strum patterns which can be used to play thousands of different songs.

This sign ⌈ is called a strum bar and indicates to strum a chord one time (usually down). Two strum bars connected with a beam (⌞⌟) indicate two strums to one beat (generally down up). When this sign ⊓ is written above a strum bar, it indicates to use a downstroke. This sign ∨ written above a strum bar, indicates to use an upstroke. When using the upstroke, play only the first two or three strings of the chord.

Practice strumming the following chords using the down and up strokes.

51.

This is a strum pattern ⌈ ⌞⌟ ⌈ ⌞⌟ . It is a combination of down and up strokes. When counting the strum patterns, down strums occur on the beats and are counted as the number of the beat on which they are played (1, 2, 3, etc.). Up strums usually occur between the beats and are counted as *and*. If you are strumming and tapping your foot on the beats, the up strum will occur when your foot is up. A down-up strum will usually get one beat (counted *one and*). Notice how the following strum pattern is counted.

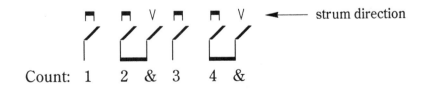

Count: 1 2 & 3 4 &

The following strum patterns can be used to play songs in 4/4 time. Each pattern takes one measure to complete. Remember, a measure is the distance between the bar lines on the staff. When you play by ear you will not be reading written music. But even if you don't have the written music showing the measures, these patterns can be applied to songs you are playing by ear. By hearing where the accents come, you can tell if the song is in 4/4 or 3/4 and feel where the measures would be.

Once you decide on the strum pattern you are going to use accompanying the song, play the same pattern in each measure. All of the patterns work for 4/4, but one may sound better for a particular song than another. The patterns are written in order of difficulty. Make sure that you have mastered one before moving to the next pattern.

Hold any chord and practice these strum patterns.

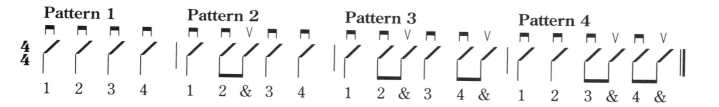

⌒ This is a tie. When it connects two strum patterns, the first strum is held through the time value of the second strum. The second strum is not played.

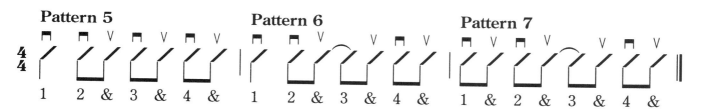

Practice the following exercises using the strum patterns for 4/4. First, in each measure play the strum pattern which is written in the first measure. Then, practice using the other strum patterns for the same exercise.

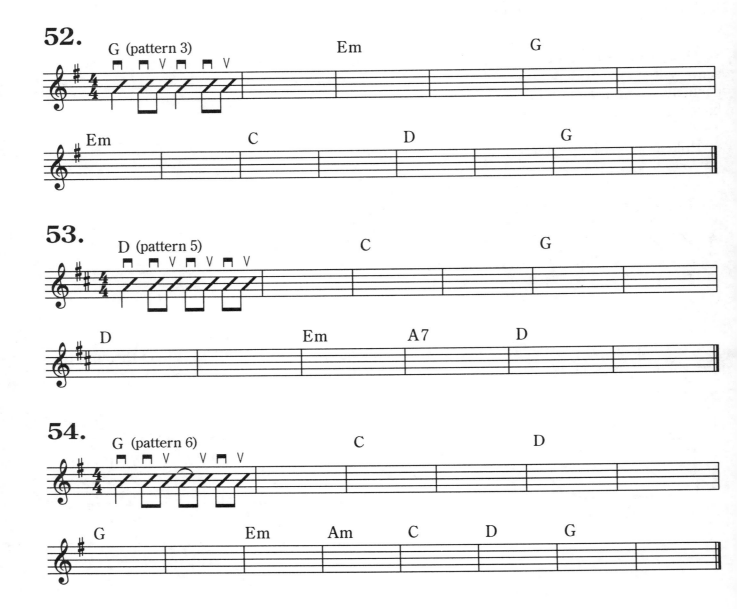

If two chords appear in a measure, the strum patterns can be divided in half, or just strum each chord two times down.

The following exercises show how two chords in a measure in 4/4 could be played. If one chord is in a measure, use the strum pattern which is written in the first measure. If two chords appear above a measure, strum them as indicated.

Practice the following chord progressions which have two chords in some of the measures.

The following strum patterns can be used to play songs in 3/4 time. Again, each pattern takes one measure to complete. Hold any chord and try these patterns.

Patterns for 3/4 meter:

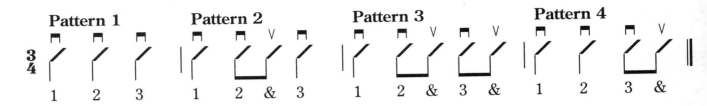

Play the following exercises in 3/4 by first using the strum pattern which is written in the first measure to play each measure and then try the other 3/4 patterns. Remember, once you have selected a strum pattern to use for the song, play the same pattern in each measure.

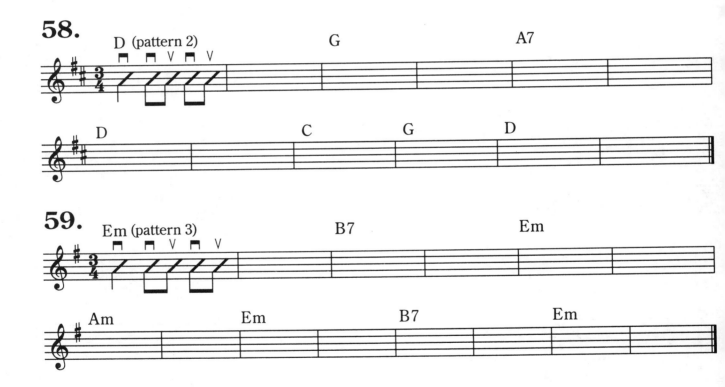

If two chords appear in a measure in 3/4 time, strum the chord which gets most of the space in the measure two times, and the other chord once.

Practice the following progressions which are in 3/4 and have some measures which contain two chords.

60.

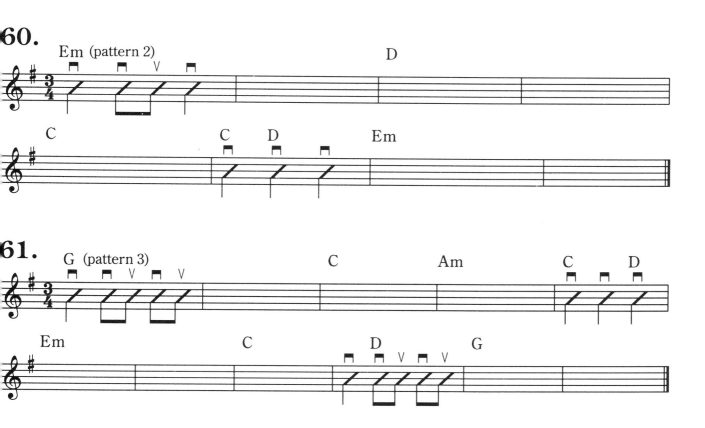

61.

The following strum patterns can be used to play music in 6/8 and 12/8 time. Hold any chord and practice these patterns.

Accent mark. In $\frac{6}{8}$, accent beats one and four.

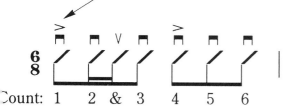

Count: 1   2 & 3   4   5   6

In 6/8 and 12/8 the eighth note strum gets one beat and the sixteenth note strum gets 1/2 beat.

In $\frac{12}{8}$, accent beats one, four, seven and ten.

Count: 1   2 & 3   4   5   6   7   8 & 9   10   11   12

Play the exercises in 6/8 and 12/8 which are written below. In each measure of the exercise, play the pattern which is written in the first measure to play each measure.

62.

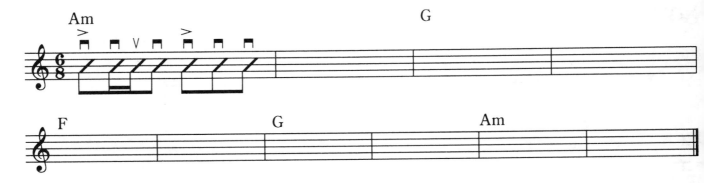

63.

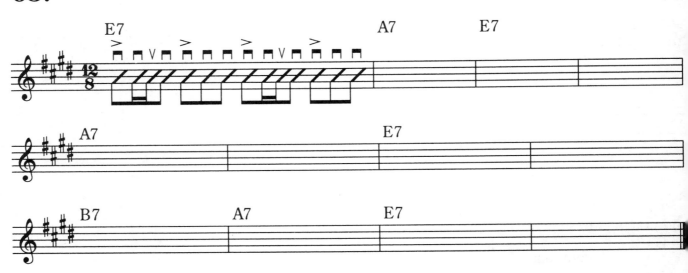

Apply the strum patterns which you have learned to songs you are playing by ear.

Pick-Strum Accompaniment Patterns

THE STYLE OF accompaniment which you will be learning in this section of the book is sometimes referred to as *pick-strum* style. It is also somtimes called *alternating bass* or *Carter style*. This is a very popular accompaniment style in country and folk music. Like the strum patterns, these patterns can be used to play thousands of songs in 4/4 and 3/4.

To learn this style, divide chords into three basic groups: 6-string chords (those for which you strum 6 strings), 5-string chords (5 strings are strummed), and 4-string chords (4 strings are strummed). The following pattern shows the pick-style accompaniment patterns for one measure of 4/4 time for a 6-string chord. The numbers represent strings which are to be picked. The strum bars indicate to strum the chord once. After the single string has been picked, you can either go back and include that string in the strum, or strum the remaining strings after the single string is picked. Hold a G chord and try the following pattern.

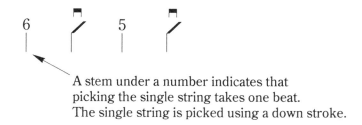

A stem under a number indicates that
picking the single string takes one beat.
The single string is picked using a down stroke.

The next pattern is for one measure of a 5-string chord. Hold a C and try this pattern.

The next pattern works for one measure of a 4-string chord. Hold a D chord and try this pattern.

Hold an F chord and try the same pattern. For the 4-string F chord, after playing the 4 ⌐, move the left hand 3rd finger to the 5th string 3rd fret to play the 5 ⌐.

Practice the following progressions using the pick-strum style. In each measure, use the correct pattern for the chord being played. (6-string patterns for 6-string chords, etc.). The patterns have been written in some of the measures to give you the idea. Play the patterns one time in each measure.

64.

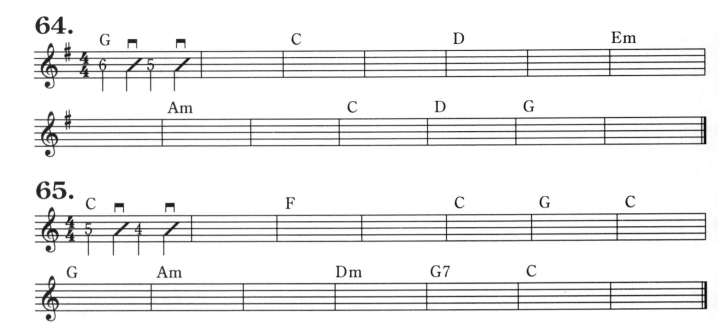

If two chords appear in a measure, play the first half of the pattern for the first chord and then play the first half of the pattern for the second chord in the measure. If C and G appear in the same measure, they will be played as written below.

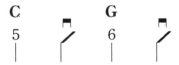

Practice the following progressions which have some measures with two chords.

66.

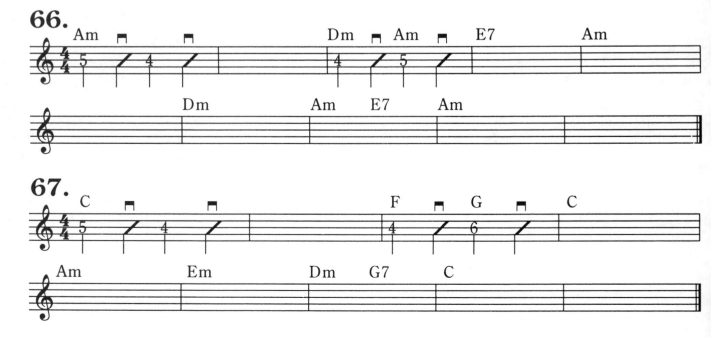

There are many variations on this style. One of the variations is written below. In the pattern for the 6-string chords, the 5 from the old pattern has been replaced with a 4. Hold a 6-string chord and try this pattern.

5-string chords (such as Am) may also be played 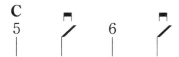. If the C chord is being played, after the ⁵│ 𝄐, move the 3rd finger of the left hand to the 6th string, 3rd fret to play the ⁶│ 𝄐. Then, move it back to the 5th string to play the ⁵│ 𝄐.

Another variation of the pick-strum style would be to replace the down strums with down-up strums. The patterns for the 6-, 5- and 4-string chords are shown below. Hold some 6-, 5- and 4-string chords and practice these patterns.

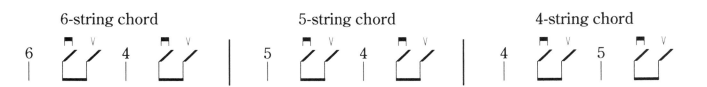

6-string chord   5-string chord   4-string chord

Practice the following progression using the variations on the pick-strum style.

68.

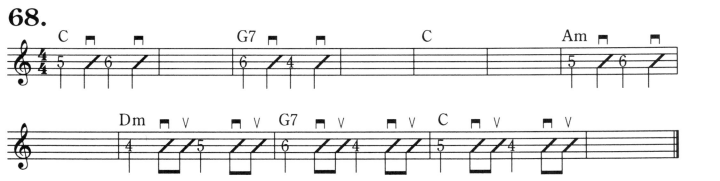

The pick-strum style can also be used to play songs in 3/4 time (actually it would be a pick-strum-strum pattern). The 3/4 patterns for the 6-, 5- and 4-string chords are written below. Hold any 6-, 5- and 4-string chords and practice these patterns.

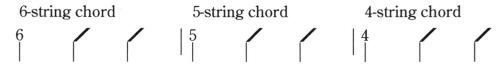

Practice the following progressions using the 3/4 patterns. Remember, play one pattern in each measure.

69.

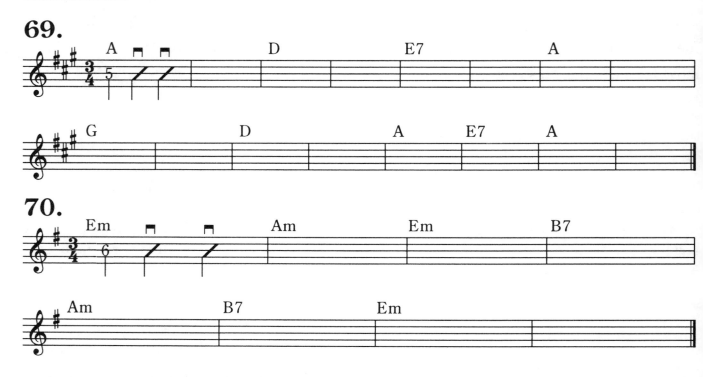

70.

A common variation on the 3/4 patterns is to substitute a down-up strum for the first down strum. These patterns are written below. Hold any 6-, 5- and 4-string chords and practice these patterns.

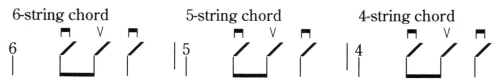

Practice the following progression using the 3/4 variation. Remember, use a 6-, 5- or 4-string pattern depending on what the chord is for the measure.

71.

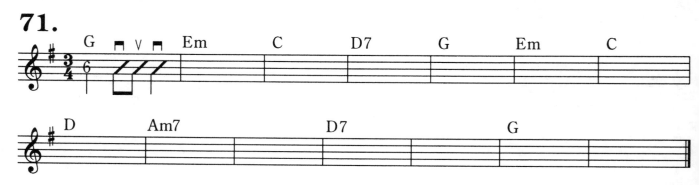

Fingerpicking Patterns

ANOTHER POPULAR STYLE of accompaniment is *fingerpicking*. On the chart below, the circled numbers to the left are for reference for the various styles of fingerpicking. Patterns ① – ④ can be used to play songs in 4/4. Patterns ① – ④ are commonly referred to as *Travis* style fingerpicking patterns (named after Merle Travis). In the Travis style of fingerpicking, the thumb plays on the beat and alternates between two bass notes. Patterns ⑤ – ⑦ can be used for slow songs in 4/4. Patterns ⑧ – ⑩ are used for songs in 3/4. The numbers on the chart below represent strings to be picked. If two numbers are written on top of each other, play those strings at the same time (the right hand middle finger will usually play the top number). The fingerpicking patterns for the 6-string chords are written in the column on the left. The 5-string patterns are written in the middle column and the patterns for the 4-string chords are written in the column on the right. The right hand fingering is written under the patterns for the 6-string chords and rhythm for the pattern is written under the patterns for the 5-string chords. For the right hand fingerings: p = thumb, i = index finger, m = middle finger, and a = ring finger. Each pattern takes one measure to complete. The right hand fingering and the rhythm is the same for the 6-, 5- and 4-string patterns of a style. For example, if you are playing a song in 4/4, and you have selected fingerpick style number ②, the right hand fingering (p – p i p m p i)and the rhythm (1 – 2 & 3 & 4 &) is the same for the 6-, 5- and 4-string chord patterns.

Here is an example of how to use the chart. Suppose you are playing a song in 4/4 time and the chord you are playing is a C. Because you are playing in 4/4, fingerpicking styles ① – ⑧ will work (some may be better than others depending on whether the song is slow or fast). Let's say you've decided to use fingerpicking style number ②. The pattern for a 5-string chord in this style goes 5 – 4 3 5 2 4 3. The 5th and 4th strings are played with the thumb, the 3rd string is played with the index (first) finger, and the 2nd string is played with the middle (second) finger. The rhythm of the pattern is 1 – 2 & 3 & 4 &. This pattern takes one measure to complete. After playing the C chord, go to the next measure and play the pattern for style number ② for a 6-, 5- and 4-string chord depending on which chord is next.

Hold any chord and practice these fingerpicking patterns. Remember, the chord you're holding is a 6-, 5- or 4-string chord depending on how many strings you strum for that chord.

6 – String Chords	5 – String Chords	4 – String Chords
4/4 ① 6 2 4 3 6 2 4 3 p m p i p m p i (fingering)	5 2 4 3 5 2 4 3 1 & 2 & 3 & 4 & (rhythm)	4 1 3 2 4 1 3 2
4/4 ② 6 – 4 3 6 2 4 3 p p i p m p i	5 – 4 3 5 2 4 3 1 2 & 3 & 4 &	4 – 3 2 4 1 3 2

6 – String Chords	5 – String Chords	4 – String Chords

$\frac{4}{4}$ ③
```
       1 ← (m, 2nd finger)
6 - 4 3 6 2 4 3
p    p i p m p i
```
```
1
5 - 4 3 5 2 4 3
1   2 & 3 & 4 &
```
```
1
4 - 3 2 4 1 3 2
```

$\frac{4}{4}$ ④
```
      1
6 - 4 - 6 2 4 3
p   p   p m p i
```
```
      1
5 - 4 - 5 2 4 3
1   2   3 & 4 &
```
```
    1
4 - 3 - 4 1 3 2
```

$\frac{4}{4}$ ⑤
```
6 4 3 2 6 4 3 2
p p i m p p i m
```
```
5 4 3 2 5 4 3 2
1 & 2 & 3 & 4 &
```
```
4 3 2 1 4 3 2 1
```

$\frac{4}{4}$ ⑥
```
1
6 4 3 2 6 4 3 2
p p i m p p i m
```
```
1
5 4 3 2 5 4 3 2
1 & 2 & 3 & 4 &
```
```
1
4 3 2 1 4 3 2 1
```

$\frac{4}{4}$ ⑦
```
    2 ← m → 2
6 4 3 4 6 4 3 4
p p i p p p i p
```
```
    2       2
5 4 3 4 5 4 3 4
1 & 2 & 3 & 4 &
```
```
    1       1
4 3 2 3 4 3 2 4
```

$\frac{3}{4}$ ⑧
```
6 4 3 2 4 3
p p i m p i
```
```
5 4 3 2 4 3
1 & 2 & 3 &
```
```
4 3 2 1 3 2
```

$\frac{3}{4}$ ⑨
```
1
6 4 3 2 4 3
p p i m p i
```
```
1
5 4 3 2 4 3
1 & 2 & 3 &
```
```
1
4 3 2 1 3 2
```

$\frac{3}{4}$ ⑩
```
    2   2
6 4 3 4 3 4
p p i p i p
```
```
    2   2
5 4 3 4 3 4
1 & 2 & 3 &
```
```
    1   1
4 3 2 3 2 3
```

   If two chords appear in a measure, divide the fingerpicking patterns and use part of each chord's pattern.

   After you have decided which style of fingerpick to use, use the same style pattern throughout the entire exercise or song.

Practice the following progressions using fingerpicking patterns. An example of a fingerpicking style from the previous page which would work for that exercise is written in the first measure. Use this pattern first and then try some of the other patterns. If the exercise is in 4/4, be sure to use patterns for 4/4, and use the patterns for 3/4 for the exercises in 3/4. Remember, each pattern takes one measure to complete.

These fingerpicking patterns can be used to play thousands of songs in 4/4 and 3/4. They can be applied to songs from songbooks, sheet music, and the songs you will be playing by ear. All you have to know is if the chord you are playing is a 6-, 5- or 4-string chord and then use the appropriate pattern for that chord.

Practice playing the songs in this book and other songs by ear, using the strum patterns, pick-strum patterns and fingerpicking patterns you have learned. First, determine if the song is in 4/4 or 3/4, then use the pattern of your choice to accompany the song.

One Chord Songs

Are You Sleeping
Farmer in the Dell
Little Tom Tinker
Row, Row, Row Your Boat
Shortnin' Bread
Sing, Sing Together

Swing Low, Sweet Chariot
Taps
There's a Hole in my Bucket
Three Blind Mice
Zum Gali Gali

Songs With Two Chords – I and V7

Adam in the Garden
A Hunting We Will Go
Alouette
Aunt Rhody
Battle of Jericho (Em B7)
Billy Boy
Blow the Man Down
Buffalo Gal
Clementine
Come Back Liza
Cuckoo Sings, The
Deaf Woman's Courtship
Deep in the Heart of Texas
D'Ou Viens-Tu, Bergere?
Doggy in the Window
Down by the Riverside *(Refrain only)*
Down by the Station
Down in the Valley
Erie Canal, The
Ezekiel Saw the Wheel
Farmer in the Deli
Go In and Out the Window
Hear Dem Bells
He's Got the Whole World in His Hands
Hot Cross Buns
Hot Time in the Old Town
Polly Wolly Doodle
Poor Little Bug
Put Your Little Foot
Rock-a My Soul
Rounds (Most of Them)
Shoo Fly
Shortnin' Bread
Skip to my Lou
Slumber Song (Schubert)

Hush Little Baby
I Know the Lord
Goodnight Irene
Jack Was Every Inch a Sailor
Keel Row, The
La Cucaracha
La Paloma
Lavender Blue
Lightly Row
Listen to the Mocking Bird
Liza Jane
London Bridge
Long, Long Ago
Lukey's Boat
Mary Had a Little Lamb
Michael Finnigan
Molly Malone
More We Get Together
Mulberry Bush
Nobody Knows the Trouble I've Seen
Oats, Peas, Beans and Barley
Old Ark's A-Moverin'
Old Blue
Old Chisholm Trail
Old Texas
Owl, The
Paw Paw Patch
Sweetly Sings the Donkey
Ten Little Indians
This Old Man
Three Blind Mice
Tom Dooley
We Are Marching to Pretoria
Where, Oh Where Has My Little Dog Gone?
Yellow Rose of Texas

Songs With Three Chords – I, IV, V7 (plus I7)

Aikin Drum
All Through the Night
Aloha Oe
America
Annie Laurie
Auld Lang Syne
Away in a Manger

Battle Hymn of the Republic
Beautiful Dreamer
Big Rock Candy Mountain
Bill Bailey
Blowing in the Wind
Boil That Cabbage Down
Botany Bay

Three Chord Songs *(continued)*

Bonnie Dundee
Bowery, The
Brahm's Lullaby
Brandy
Bring Me A Rose
Brush Those Tears From Your Eyes
Bury Me Beneath The Willow
Caisson Song
Campbells Are Coming, The
Camptown Races, The
Dry Bones
Dummy Line, The
Dying Cowboy, The
En Roulant Ma Boule
Everybody Loves A Lover
First Noel
For the Beauty of the Earth
Four Strong Winds
Frankie and Johnny
Get On Board
Goin' Down the Road
Goin' to Build a Mountain
Golden Slippers
Goodby My Lover
Goodnight Ladies
Grandfather's Clock
Great Gettin' Up Morning
Green, Green Grass of Home
Gypsy Rover
Halls of Montezuma
Ham and Eggs
Haul on the Bowlin'
Hand Me Down My Walking Cane
Happy Birthday
Happy Wanderer, The (Falderee)
Hard Ain't It Hard
Hear Dem Bells
He's a Jolly Good Fellow
Hensies
Hill and Gully
Hobo's Lullaby
Hole 'Em Joe
Holly and the Ivy, The
Home on the Range
Hundred Pipers
Lemon Tree
Let My Little Light Shine
Li'l Liza Jane
Limericks
Little Annie Rooney
Little Brown Church in the Vale
Little Brown Jug
Lock Lomand
Lonesone Valley
Lord, I Want to Be a Christian

Lots of Fish in Bonavist'
Love is a Gentle Thing
Magic Penny
Maid of Amsterdam, The
Mama Don't Allow
Mandy
Marianne (All Day)
Mary and Martha
Matilda
Me and Bobby McGee
Melody D'Amour
Michael Rowed the Boat Ashore
Midnight Special
Mocking Bird, The
Moonlight Bay
M.T.A.
Muffin Man
Music in the Air
My Bonnie
My Heart Cries for You
My Truly Fair
Nearer My God to Thee
Nellie Gray
Nelly Bly
Noah's Ark
Nobody Knows the Trouble I've Seen
Roll, Jordan, Roll
Roll on Columbia
Ronde de L'Amour (Oscar Strauss)
Running
Saints Go Marching
Sally Brown
Sam Gone Away
Santa Lucia
Sentimental Journey
Seven Joys of Mary
She'll Be Comin' Round the Mountain
Sidewalks of New York
Silent Night
Silver Bells
Sixteen Miles
Sleep, Baby, Sleep
Sloop John B.
Snowbird (D.A.E.)
So Long, It's Been Good to Know You
Some Folks Do
Streets of Laredo
Supercalifragilisticexpialidocious
Swanee River
Swing Low
Take Me to the Sweet Sunny South
Talking Blues
Tavern in the Town
That's What Happiness Is
There's a Hole in My Bucket

Three Chord Songs *(continued)*

There Are Many Flags in Many Lands
There's Music in the Air
There Stands a Little Man
This Land is Your Land
Canadien Errant, Un
Can't You Dance the Polka
Catch a Falling Star
Cherry Tree Carol
Chiapanecas
Church in the Wildwood
Cielito Lindo
Cindy
Comin's Round the Mountain
Comin's Through the Rye
Cradle Song (Mozart)
Crawdad Song
Dans Tous Les Cantons
Deck the Halls
The Fox
Desperado
Diggin' on the New Railroad
Dinah (In the Kitchen)
Du! Du! Liegst Mir Im Herzen
Done Laid Around
Donkey Riding
Don't It Make You Want to Go Home
Down by the Riverside
Drink to Me Only With Thine Eyes
I Couldn't Hear Nobody Pray
If I Had a Hammer
If I Were Free
I Gave My Love a Cherry
I Know the Lord
I'm On My Way
In Bright Mansions Above
In the King's Garden
Irene Goodnight
I Saw Three Ships
I'se the B'ye
I Think of You
It Is No Secret What God Can Do
I've Been Working On the Railroad
I've Got Sixpence
I Wish I Were Single Again!
Jacob's Ladder
Jamaica Farewell
Jimmie Crack Corn
Jingle Bells
John Brown's Body
John B's Sails, The
John Jacob Jinglheimer Schmidt
John Peel
Jolly Good Fellow
Joy to the World
Juanita
Jump Down, Spin Around

Just a Closer Walk With Thee
Kathleen Aroon
Keel Row, The
Kum Ba Yah
La Cucaracha
Last Night I Had the Strangest Dream
Last Thing On My Mind
Oh! Bury Me Not on the Lone Prairie
Oh! Dear What Can the Matter Be?
Oh! Freedom
Oh! Lord I'm Tired
Oh! Mary Don't You Weep
Oh! Susanna!
Oh! Tannenbaum
O! Dan Tucker
Old Black Joe
Old Chisholm Trail
Old Cotton Fields Back Home
Old Folks at Home
Old Gray Mare, The
Old Kentucky Home
Old MacDonald
Old Oaken Bucket
Old Paint (Ride Around)
Old Rugged Cross
Old Time Religion
Oleanna
One More River
On Top of Old Smokey
Over the River
Pack Up Your Sorrows
Publ With No Beer
Quilting Party
Rancho Grande
Rambling Baoy
Red River Valley
Reuben and Rachel
Ring, Ring the Banjo
Rio Grande
Road to the Isles
Rock of Ages
Rolling Home
This Train
Those Brown Eyes
Trail to Pretoria
Tie Me Kangaroo Down Sport
Turkey in the Straw
Twinkle, Twinkle Little Star
Two of Us, The
Unicorn, The
Vive la Canadienne
Vive L'Amour
Wabash Cannonball
Wait for the Wagon
Wand'ring Minstrel, A
Waterbound

Three Chord Songs *(continued)*

Wearin' O' the Green, The
Wee Cooper of Fife
We'll Rant and We'll Roar
We'll Sing in the Sunshine
Whispering Hope
Wide River

Worried Man Blues
Wreck of John B.
Yankee Doodle
Yellow Bird
You Are My Sunshine

Songs With Four Chords – I, IV, II7, V7, (plus I7)

Anchors Aweigh
Away in a Manger
Bells of St. Mary's
Bill Bailey
Caissons Go Rolling
Carry Me Back to Old Virginny
Casey Jones
Cockles and Mussels
Coulter's Candy
Daisy a Day, A
Daisy, Daisy!
Dixie
Double Mint Gum
Good Old Summertime
Green, Green
He's a Jolly Good Fellow
Hey, What About Me?
Home on the Range
I Got Shoes
I Love a Lassie
In the Good Old Summertime
Irene Goodnight
I've Been Working on the Railroad
I've Got to Know
I Want to Be Ready
Jingle Bells
Click Go the Shears

Waltzing Matilda
Killegrew's Soiree
Last Thing On My Mind (VII, V)
Long, Long Trail
Lovely Bunch of Coconuts
Lover's Concerto (Bach's Minuet in G)
MacNamara's Band
Massa's in the Cold, Cold Ground
My Bonnie
Oh! Mary Don't You Weep
Oh! Susanna!
Old Gray Bonnet
Our Boys Will Shine Tonight
Puff the Magic Dragon
Put You Hand in the Hand (IIm)
Ramblin' Rose
Road to Gundagai
Roamin's in the Gloamin'
Rudolf the Red Nosed Reindeer
Shortnin' Bread
Sugar in the Morning
Swanee River
Time Passes
Twelve Days of Christmas
Wearin' O' the Green
Wild Irish Rose
Winchester Cathedral

Chord Reference Section

THE FOLLOWING DIAGRAMS show dozens of fingerings for chords positioned in the first four frets of the guitar. Many of them use open strings. The chords have been grouped in categories according to their type (*i.e.,* major, minor, 7, maj7, etc.). If you need help finding a chord which is not on these sheets, refer to the section in this book on Barre Chords.

Major Chords

A	Bb	B	C	D

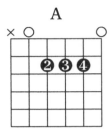 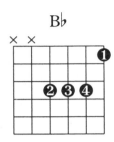 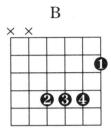 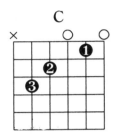 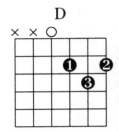

the first finger lays across two strings

E	F	G

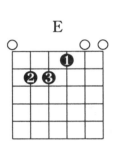 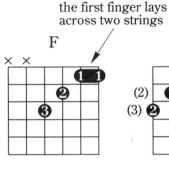 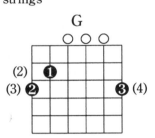

Minor Chords

Am	Bm	Cm	Dm	Em

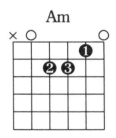 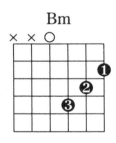 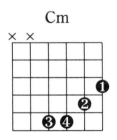 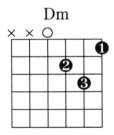 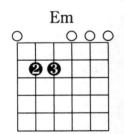

Fm	Gm

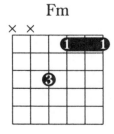 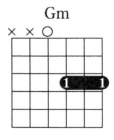

Seventh Chords
(7)

A7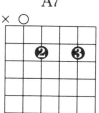

B7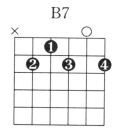

C7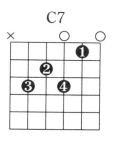

D7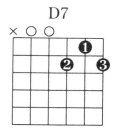

E7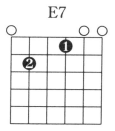

E7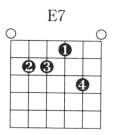

F7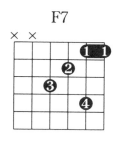

G7

Major Seventh Chords (maj7 – Major sevenths may also be written 7̄ or Δ)

Amaj7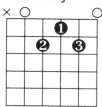

Cmaj7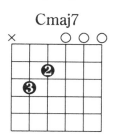

Dmaj7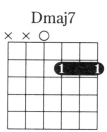

Emaj7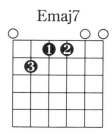

Fmaj7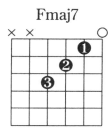

Gmaj7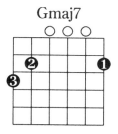

Minor Seventh Chords (m7)

Am7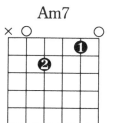

Am7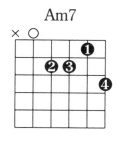

Dm7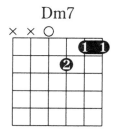

Em7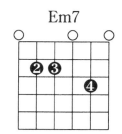

Em7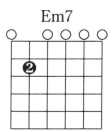

Major Sixth Chords (6)

A6
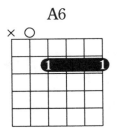

C6
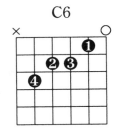

D6
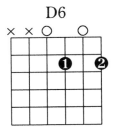

E6
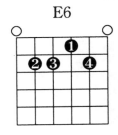

F6
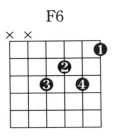

G6
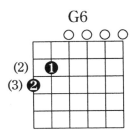

Suspended Chords (sus)

Asus
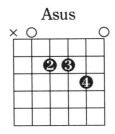

Csus
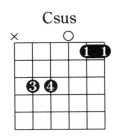

Dsus
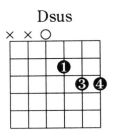

Esus
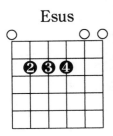

Fsus
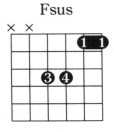

Gsus
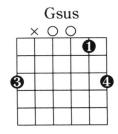

The x's above these two diagrams indicate that the left-hand, third finger is to be tilted and lightly touch the fifth string. The fifth string should be dead.

Seventh Suspended Chords (7sus)

A7sus
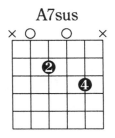

C7sus
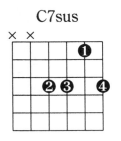

D7sus
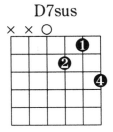

E7sus
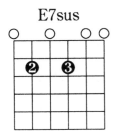

G7sus
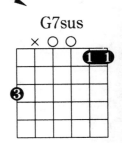

Add Nine Chords (add9)

Aadd9
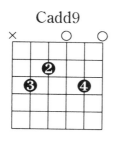

Cadd9
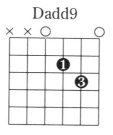

Dadd9
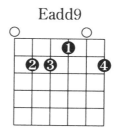

Eadd9
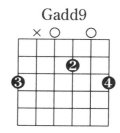

Gadd9

Diminished Seventh Chords (dim or °)

Cdim (D♯dim, A dim, F♯°)
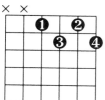

C♯dim (Edim, B♭dim, G°)
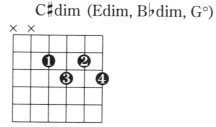

The diminished seventh chord can have four letter names for the same pattern. Every finger is on a note which names the chord.

Augmented Chords (aug or +)

Faug (C♯aug, A+)
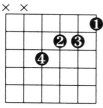

The augmented chord can have three letter names for the same pattern. Here again, each finger is on a note which names the chord.